# SKY

## the Deaf

# HOME RUN HERO

### A LESSON IN COURAGE

Written By: Mickey Carolan

Third Culture Books

An imprint of Third Culture Books LLC

Michigan

Most Portfolio books are available at a discount when purchased in large quantities. For more information please email mickey@mickeycarolan.com.

Published by Third Culture Books.

Illustration Design by Adisa Fazlovic

ISBN: 979-8-9879923-0-2 (Hardcover)
ISBN: 979-8-9879923-1-9 (Paperback)
ISBN: 979-8-9879923-2-6 (ebook)

Printed in the United States of America

# Dedication

I lovingly dedicate this
book to my family.

This story was inspired by my late
father, Sky, to whom sports were a
great equalizer.

Cheers to parents in both the Deaf
and Hearing communities.
Keep doing the best you can,
because we have
the BEST JOB
in the world!

This is

 SKY.

Sky was born Deaf.
He loved playing
baseball and being
Deaf didn't stop
him from doing
what he loved the
most.

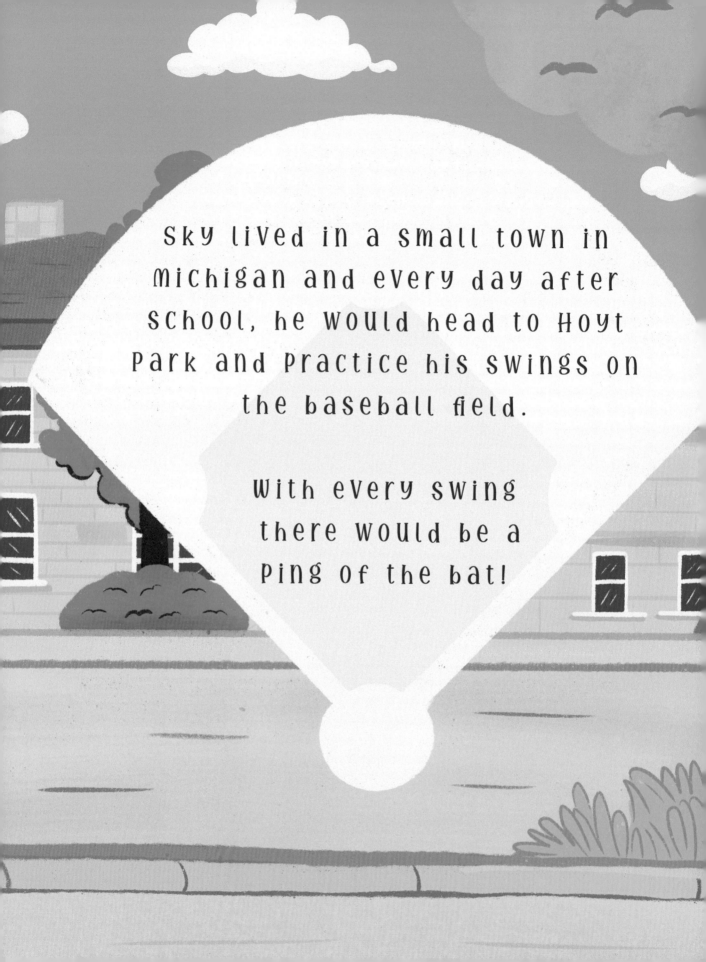

Sky lived in a small town in Michigan and every day after school, he would head to Hoyt Park and practice his swings on the baseball field.

With every swing there would be a ping of the bat!

One day, as Sky was
practicing, a strange
thing happened.

Every time he hit the
ball, it would fly out of
the park and disappear
into the sky like a
soaring eagle.-

At first, Sky thought it was just luck, but it happened again and again.

Sky soon realized that he had a superpower – not hearing allowed Sky to focus on the ball better and hit home runs with ease!

Sky was overjoyed with his new power, but he also knew that he had to use it for good.

He declared, "With every home run a bully becomes a friend!"

In turn, a group of bullies were picking on his brothers Marc and Colt.

Sky stepped in to help. Sky didn't communicate very clearly verbally, and the bullies mocked him and stole Colt's baseball.

Sky saw that Colt
was visibly upset
and crying over
having his
baseball stolen.

The next day, while walking home alone from school Sky saw the bullies again.
And again, they mocked him, and this time they stole his baseball glove!
Sky yelled and signed **"STOP"** to the bullies, but they still stole his baseball glove.

Then Opening Day
arrived at Hoyt Park!

Sky was excited
because this was his
first year of being
on an organized
baseball team.

When Sky and his
brothers showed up to
the park their team was
scheduled to play the bullies.

And the bullies didn't
take Sky seriously at first, but
when he hit the ball out of the
park,
they were amazed.

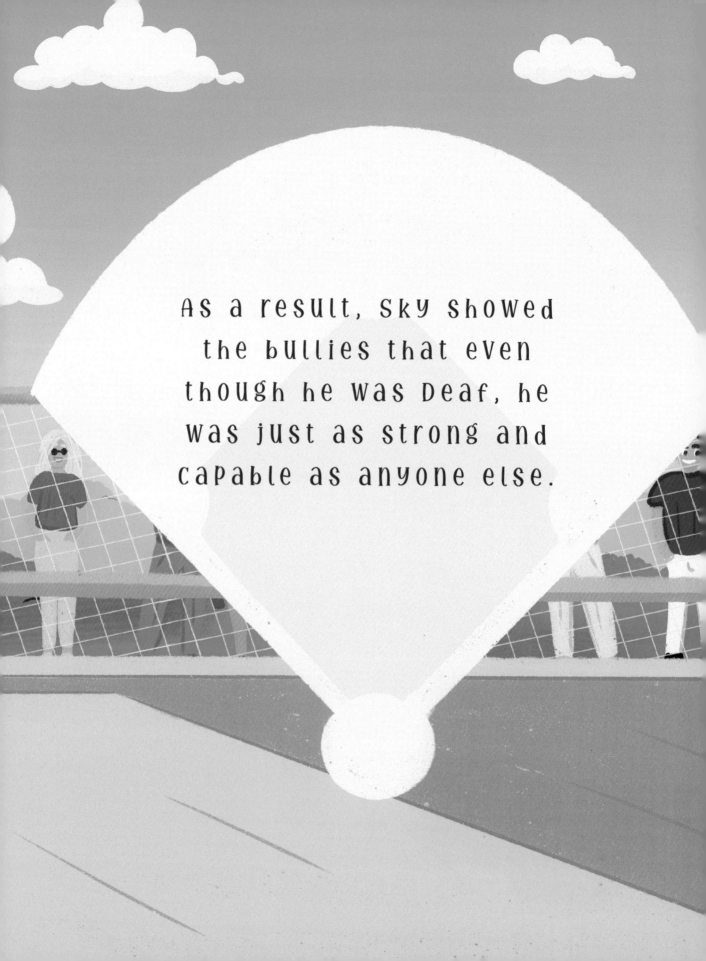

As a result, Sky showed the bullies that even though he was Deaf, he was just as strong and capable as anyone else.

From that day on,
the bullies left Sky and his
friends alone.
Sky became known as the "Home run
Hero" throughout the town.
His nickname gave him grand slam
sized courage to stand up to bullies!
Sky continued to use
his power to help others
and make the world
a better place.

And even though he was Deaf, he could still see the cheers of the crowds and feel the joy of hitting a home run in his heart.

# Batter UP:
# Free Bonus Post-Reading Gift Idea

1. Courage Crew: Research 2-4 famous athletes who have special needs like Sky. How do they show resilience and courage?

2. The Sky's The Limit: Write a postcard to Sky about his ability to use his deafness as superpower. How does he show heroism?

3. Antibully Box: Make a box and fill it with items that encourage other kids or teens to show kindness, not bullying. What items can you suggest? Why?

4. My Super Power: Reflect on your own life. Identify one aspect that makes you unique from others and how it serves as your own superpower.

5. Take a Stand: How can you help others to take a stand against bullying? Formulate 2-4 ideas for your school or community.

# About the author

Children's author Mickey Carolan did not have to look far for inspiration for his new picture book, Sky, the Deaf Home Run Hero: A Lesson in Courage. Being raised by two deaf parents motivated Mickey to share his family's story as a legacy for future generations and as a social emotional learning message for all children in the deaf community

As a CODA, or child of a deaf adult, and with American Sign Language as his first language, Mickey witnessed first-hand the challenges that face some deaf children, namely being bullied for being different. It was important for him to create a book in which a deaf child can see themselves in the story and how they can make a difference. He wants his young readers—deaf and hearing—to come away from his story understanding that deaf children can do anything except hear and that this stays with them long after the book is closed.

Mickey lives outside Grand Rapids, Michigan, with his wife, Erin and their two children, Elloree and Brooks. When he isn't writing stories of courage and resilience for children, Mickey enjoys spending time with his family, coaching youth sports, reading, and lifting weights. Sky, the Deaf Home Run Hero: A Lesson in Courage is his debut children's book, the first installment in the Deaf Kids Can series.